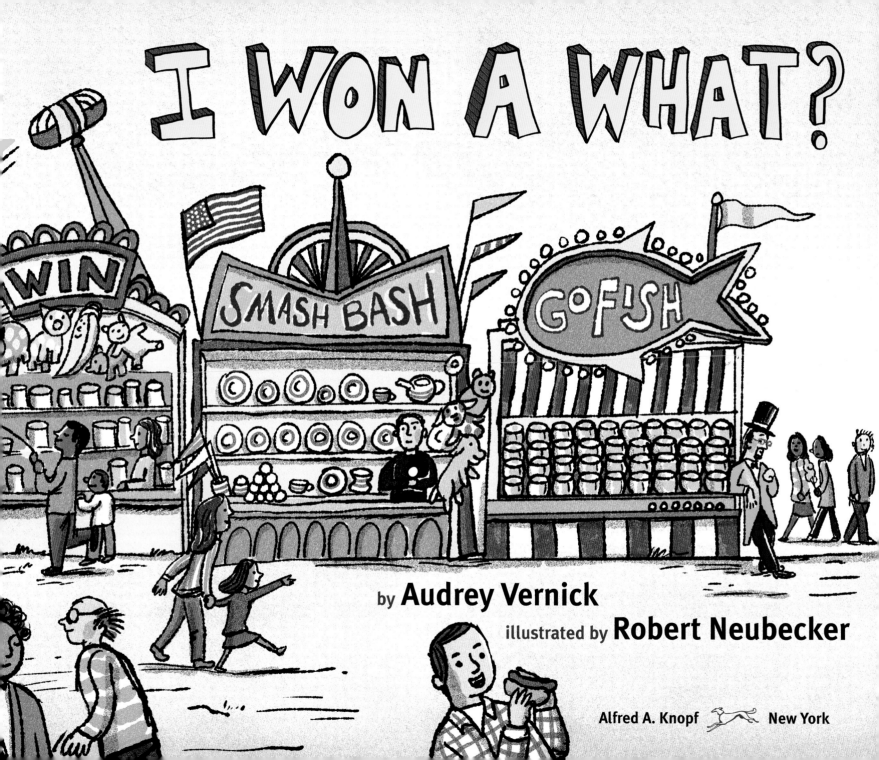

I WON A WHAT?

WIN

SMASH BASH

GOFISH

by **Audrey Vernick**

illustrated by **Robert Neubecker**

Alfred A. Knopf   New York

I have to win this goldfish.

My parents won't let me have anything fluffy.

Or shaggy. Or feathery. Or that eats mice.

"We're just being practical," they say.

They are always being practical.

But finally, tonight, they say I can keep anything I win at the goldfish booth!

I have just one more chance.

"Where's my goldfish?" I ask.

"You didn't win a goldfish," the booth guy says.

"You won Nuncio!"

Nuncio, it turns out, is bigger than a goldfish.

Or a dog. Or a goat.

Or a baby elephant.

Or a refrigerator.

I won a whale!

"This is impossible," Mom says.

"It's impractical," Dad says.

"But you promised!" I say.

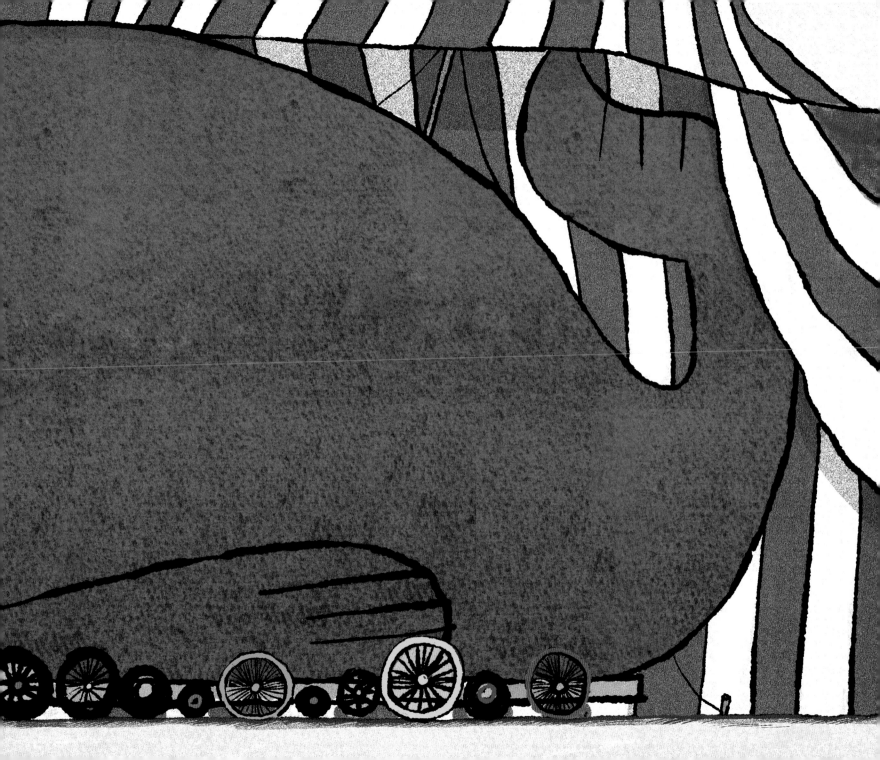

My parents are practical.
But they are also very, very fair.
"We can try it out," Dad says.
"On a trial basis," Mom says.

We fill our enormous swimming pool with salt water until it's just right for Nuncio.

I've always wanted something I could take care of. Something that loves me back. Maybe that was a lot to ask of a goldfish. But a whale! A whale seems capable of almost anything!

Nuncio swims right up to me when I bring his lunch. I tell him about school while he eats. He is an excellent listener.

I hear . . . well, at first I think it's a musical cow.

Or a broken, slowed-down siren.

Possibly a hurt donkey.

But it's Nuncio!

We take Nuncio to the ocean for a swim. I can tell we have
a lot in common, though I don't have a blowhole.

The only thing I don't love about Nuncio is cleaning his pool.

It's complicated. And takes a really long time.

But it's worth it. Because once the pool's clean, Nuncio jumps way up, spins in the air, then dives right back in. I don't know what it means, but it's beautiful.

"This isn't working out," Dad says.
And that's when I realize something
about Nuncio.

Not only is he a great swimmer. And a good listener. And
an enthusiastic eater. And able to sing like a musical cow.

Nuncio can be practical!
I get him started helping
Dad in the garden.

Mom washes her car in record time
with Nuncio's help.

And at the end of a long, hot day, he helps us all cool down.

"He's surprising, that whale of yours," Mom says.

"A real keeper," Dad says.

Nuncio and I agree.

I guess I would have learned to like a goldfish.

But I think maybe I was meant to love a whale.

I wonder what he thinks about me.

Our pod's firstborn has brought so much more than I ever hoped for.
For Jacob, whom I watch with joy and awe. —A.V.

For Isidore! —R.N.

THIS IS A BORZOI BOOK PUBLISHED BY ALFRED A. KNOPF

Text copyright © 2016 by Audrey Vernick

Illustrations copyright © 2016 by Robert Neubecker

All rights reserved. Published in the United States by Alfred A. Knopf, an imprint of Random House Children's Books,
a division of Penguin Random House LLC, New York.

Knopf, Borzoi Books, and the colophon are registered trademarks of Penguin Random House LLC.

Visit us on the Web! randomhousekids.com

Educators and librarians, for a variety of teaching tools, visit us at RHTeachersLibrarians.com

Library of Congress Cataloging-in-Publication Data

Vernick, Audrey.

I won a what? / by Audrey Vernick ; illustrated by Robert Neubecker. — First edition.

pages cm.

Summary: A young boy tries to win a goldfish at the carnival and ends up with a far bigger prize.

ISBN 978-0-553-50993-9 (trade) — ISBN 978-0-553-50994-6 (lib. bdg.) — ISBN 978-0-553-50995-3 (ebook)

[1. Whales as pets—Fiction. 2. Pets—Fiction. 3. Humorous stories.] I. Neubecker, Robert, illustrator. II. Title.

PZ7.V5973Iam 2016 [E]—dc23 2015013259

The illustrations in this book were created using an Apple computer and a #2 pencil.

MANUFACTURED IN CHINA

April 2016   10 9 8 7 6 5 4 3 2 1   First Edition

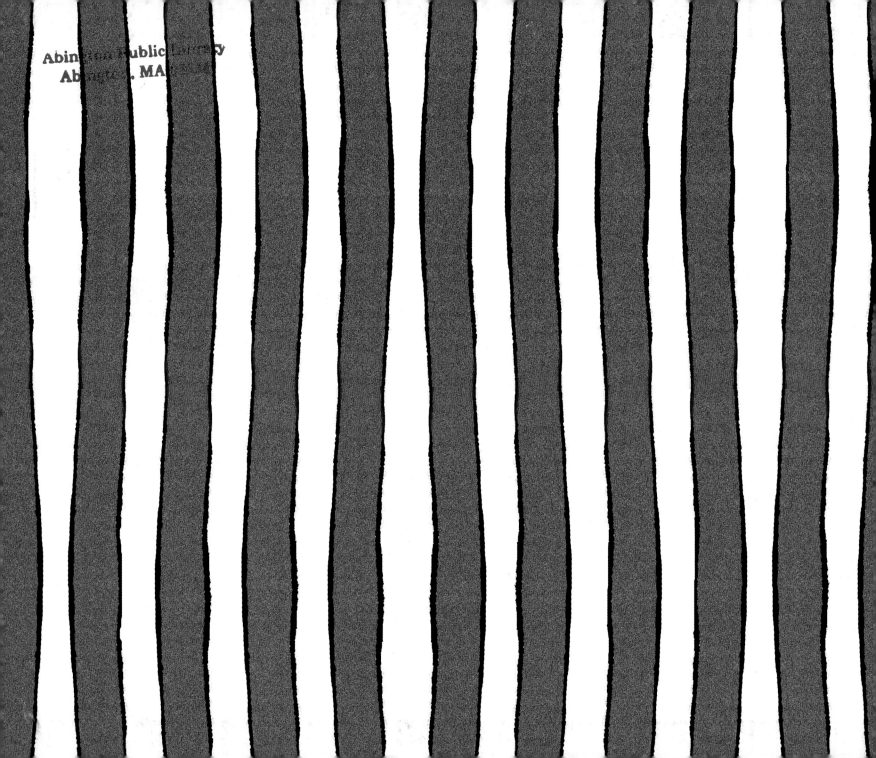